Cracked

Michele
Martin
Bossley

Orca currents

ORCA BOOK PUBLISHERS

Library and Archives Canada Cataloguing in Publication

Bossley, Michele Martin
Cracked / written by Michele Martin Bossley.
(Orca currents)
ISBN 978-1-55143-702-6 (bound)
ISBN 978-1-55143-700-2 (pbk.)
I. Title. II. Series.

PS8553.O7394C73 2007 jC813'.54 C2007-900248-X

Summary: Trevor, Nick and Courtney have to solve the mystery
of the bobsled saboteur.

First published in the United States, 2007
Library of Congress Control Number: 2007920329

Orca Book Publishers gratefully acknowledges the support for its publishing
programs provided by the following agencies: the Government of Canada
through the Book Publishing Industry Development Program and the
Canada Council for the Arts, and the Province of British Columbia through
the BC Arts Council and the Book Publishing Tax Credit.

Cover design: Doug McCaffry
Cover photography: Getty Images

Orca Book Publishers
PO Box 5626, Station B
Victoria, BC Canada
V8R 6S4

Orca Book Publishers
PO Box 468
Custer, WA USA
98240-0468

www.orcabook.com
Printed and bound in Canada.
Printed on 100% PCW recycled paper.
010 09 08 07 • 5 4 3 2 1

For Jordan and Matthew, for their continual support and enthusiasm about books and writing. I'm so proud of you both.

chapter one

Rrrr...Rrrr...Rrrr. The faint vibrations were getting louder. I shivered as a freezing gust of wind whipped across the hillside.

Courtney Gantz dug an elbow into my ribs. "Heads up, Trevor," she said. "If it's an orange sled with blue trim, it's my brother."

"We know," my cousin Nick said. He pulled his ratty toque further down over his dark hair as another blast of wind peppered us with icy snowflakes.

I watched Robyn hop up and down to keep warm and wished Courtney were someplace else. Nick, Robyn and I were all pretty good friends, but Courtney was Robyn's locker partner at school and insisted on hanging around with us. She had told us about her Olympic-caliber bobsledder brother fifty million times since our school's week at Canada Olympic Park had begun—and it was only Monday!

"I'd sure like to try this," I said with enthusiasm. Nick looked at me like I was insane.

"You have to be kidding," he said, shaking his head. Nick is tall and skinny, and would probably be awesome at basketball if he tried, which he doesn't. Sports aren't his thing.

We were standing at the Kreisel, one of the most difficult turns on the track and the best vantage point for seeing the second half of the race. It was just a practice today, and it had started late, but our teacher let us wait so we could see at least one sled make the run.

"If you want to try bobsledding, you should really talk to Josh," Courtney said. "He can tell you all about it. You'd probably start off as a brakeman—there's four-man and two-man sleds, so they always need brakemen. You have to be a really good sprinter. The bobsledders have to push that sled at the top of the track as fast as they can, then jump in just before they go down the hill. The push start can make or break a race. Josh trains at the push track all the time."

"What are you, a spokesperson for the sport?" Nick asked.

"Trevor said he was interested," Courtney shot back. "I wasn't talking to *you*."

"What's a push track?" Robyn asked. She rubbed a finger across her teeth. "I think my braces have frozen to my lips."

"Don't get her started again," Nick muttered. "I just got her to shut up."

Courtney ignored him. "It's a practice track where the athletes work on their starts. And let me tell you, those sleds weigh a ton!"

"So why is the push start such a big deal?" Robyn wanted to know. The wind whipped her brown hair across her face. "I thought that the sled just, you know, went down the hill and that was it."

"Yeah, but the more speed you have from the push start, the faster you'll go down the track," Courtney said. "Then it's up to the driver. Josh had to take special training to learn how to drive the sled. He just got to be a driver this year."

RRRR...RRRR...RRRR! The vibrations turned into a muffled roar.

"Here they come!" Courtney leaned eagerly against the railing. A blur of orange streaked past before I had a chance to see it clearly. The sled went into the turn. I watched it careering back and forth on the smooth curved ice of the track as it rocketed through the Kreisel.

"Aren't they supposed to keep the sled steady, Trevor?" asked Robyn.

"I think so," I answered. Courtney's attention was riveted to the orange sled that was fishtailing out of control.

"What's wrong?" Robyn said, just as a screech of tearing metal filled the air. Something silver had wrenched loose and was lying on the ice. The sled flipped.

"Josh!" Courtney screeched. The bobsled landed on its side and skidded toward the final turn, where it slowed to a grinding stop.

Courtney raced toward the wounded sled, ignoring all the barriers. Coaches and other track officials hurried in the same direction.

"Courtney, wait!" yelled Mr. Kowalski, our teacher. She ignored him. Mr. Kowalski sighed. "All of you, stay here! Don't move," he warned. "I have to go get her. But I want you kids well back from the accident, understand?"

We nodded as Mr. Kowalski followed Courtney. I hesitated, and then I started toward the section of track where the sled had flipped.

"Trevor! What are you doing?" Robyn called.

"There's something down there." I climbed onto one of the supports and peered down. The piece of metal, freshly torn from the sled, gleamed against the ice. I eased myself over the barrier and onto the track. I grabbed the steel runner just as my feet skidded out from under me. Like a cartoon character on a banana peel, I flailed wildly before I landed on my backside and began a slow but unstoppable descent toward the overturned bobsled.

My face flamed red. My underwear froze to my rear end. Mr. Kowalski reached across the barrier as I arrived, hoisting me over the concrete wall. "What," he said through clenched teeth, "are you doing?"

"Um...gathering evidence?" I held up the steel runner.

Mr. Kowalski groaned. "Look, Trevor. This is not the time for any detective stuff, okay? And not from you two, either," he added, glaring at Robyn and Nick, who had just run down the stairs from the Kreisel platform.

Robyn bristled at that comment, partly because the three of us had solved a major crime in the past year, but mostly because she didn't like being blamed for my bum slide down the track.

Mr. Kowalski was distracted by the bobsledders, who were easing themselves out of the sled. Courtney froze. The brakeman moved gingerly, shaking out arms and legs, before nodding that he was okay.

"I guess that's why they wear crash helmets," Robyn said.

But the driver wasn't so lucky. He held his right arm close to his body and winced when it moved. Someone helped him remove his helmet, and Courtney let her breath out in an audible gasp.

"James Ramsey!" she cried. "But where's Josh?"

The driver turned toward her. "That's what I'd like to know," Ramsey said.

"Why are you guys in his sled?" Courtney asked.

"Because our steering mechanism needs to be fixed, and Josh offered to let us use his sled for a few practice runs today," answered the driver. He caught sight of me, still holding the steel runner. His eyes narrowed. "Where did you get that?" he demanded.

"Uh...I picked it up off the track. It came off the sled during your run," I said.

At that moment, Josh arrived, breathless from running down the path from the top of the track. "What happened?" he gasped.

Ramsey took a step forward, his face menacing. "We crashed. Thanks to you."

"What are you talking about?" Josh gave him a bewildered look.

"I'm talking about this." Ramsey snatched the steel bar from me with his good hand. "Nice timing. The runner fell off during our run. Next time, loosen the bolts a little more. I only wrecked my wrist, instead of getting killed," he said sarcastically. He held the damaged arm close to his body.

"Are you saying I'd trash my own sled?" Josh bristled.

"Well, if I can't compete, you qualify for the National team. Go figure." Ramsey grimaced with pain.

"I wouldn't do that!" Josh said angrily.

"So why don't I believe you?" the driver retorted. "That runner didn't come off by itself." He tossed the piece of metal to Josh, who caught it neatly in one hand. "And when I get through with the Nationals committee, the only way you'll see a bobsled again is if you have a wide-screen TV!"

chapter two

"Are you threatening me?" Josh demanded.

"I don't have to," Ramsey said, red-faced and furious. "It's your sled. You were the last guy to touch those runners. You planned that crash, letting me drive your sled with a loose runner."

I heard Courtney draw in a sharp breath.

"That's a pretty serious accusation," Mr. Kowalski said. "How do you know it was deliberate? It could have been an accident."

"It's no accident when two athletes are neck and neck going into the National trials, and only one of us is going to World's this year." Ramsey walked away, holding his injured wrist.

Josh stared after him, the warped runner gripped tightly in one hand. One of the coaches approached him. "Josh, we're going to have to look into this. Why don't you go home, take some time off for a few days. Get some rest."

Josh's jaw dropped. "You believe that guy?"

"No, no," the coach soothed. "It's just that with an accusation like this, we have to be careful. Don't worry about it."

"What do you mean, don't worry about it? Ramsey throws this garbage at me, you suspend me from the track, and you tell me not to worry about it?" Josh said.

"I'm not suspending you. But this situation is a bit touchy. Until we get it sorted out, I think you and Ramsey should stay away from each other," the coach said.

"This is stupid. I need to practice, Coach. The National trials are coming up."

"You've been having some great runs. It's no problem for you to take a couple days off." The coach was firm.

Josh saw that there was no point arguing. "Okay." He turned and started down the hill toward the bottom of the track.

Courtney's hazel eyes filled with tears. "I can't believe they're going to kick him out. He's worked so hard to make the National team."

"They won't kick him out," Robyn said. "It was just an accident."

Courtney turned to me. "Can you guys help him?"

"Us? What do you mean?" I said.

"Well, you found out who was stealing lunches at school a few months ago. Couldn't you—I don't know—figure out what happened?"

Courtney couldn't look any less like her brother. Josh was around twenty years old and angular, with the flat muscles of a trained athlete. Like me, he had sandy

12

brown hair and wasn't overly tall. Courtney was chubby with a soft cloud of red hair. Her face was round, with curved lips and a big smile. Right now, she fixed me with a pleading expression.

"Sure, we'll help," Robyn said. "We're at Olympic Park all week anyway. Maybe we can find something out."

Courtney breathed a sigh of relief. "Thanks. I don't want my brother to go to jail or anything."

I snorted. "I don't think that's likely."

"Don't be so sure," Nick said. "There was a case about ten years ago, where a figure skater paid some guy to smash another skater's knees so she couldn't compete. It was all over the papers. Josh could get framed, even if it was just an accident. They could charge him with attempted murder!"

Courtney looked horrified.

"That's ridiculous!" said Robyn.

"I think attempted murder is going a bit far," I added.

"Think about it," Nick warned. "If the police were to find a motive...and Josh has one—he wants Ramsey out of competition—they could build a case."

"Really?" squeaked Courtney.

Nick nodded. "It's possible."

Robyn elbowed Nick in the ribs. "You're not helping," she said.

"Look, Robyn. Josh could be in real trouble. Why else would the coach tell him to stay away from the track?" Nick said. "I think we need to consider all the possibilities."

Robyn and I looked at each other. It was impossible to deny that Nick had a point.

"Come on, kids. Let's get going. The bus should be waiting for us in the parking lot by now," Mr. Kowalski called.

It was a long walk from the bobsled track to the parking lot, and we still had to get to the bottom of the track. Mr. Kowalski hurried us down the hill, and we passed Josh, who was talking to a beautiful, dark-haired woman dressed in jeans and a green sweater.

"Who's that?" I asked Courtney.

She frowned. "I have no idea. She looks familiar, though."

14

I was about to suggest that maybe Josh had a girlfriend, when I heard him say angrily, "I have nothing to say to you!"

"But, Josh, it would help you if you just said how you feel about the situation," the woman said.

"No!" Josh stamped off. The woman thrust her hands into the pockets of her sweater and stared after him, before she finally headed toward the coach.

"Secret romance?" Robyn wondered.

"Maybe not," I said thoughtfully. "I think she's a reporter. Look."

The woman had pulled a notebook out of her pocket and was scribbling rapidly as the coach spoke to her. Then James Ramsey appeared, his arm wrapped in a makeshift sling.

"How'd she get here so fast?" Robyn asked.

"The press have radio scanners," Nick answered knowledgeably. "They probably heard about the accident when the ambulance was called, and sent her over to see what was going on."

Ramsey was talking, gesturing with his good arm. I didn't like the satisfied smile on his face as the reporter took notes.

I shook my head. "I think Josh's problems are about to get even worse."

chapter three

Sabotage Alleged in Bobsled Crash
Injured driver unable to compete in
Olympic Trials

*Suspicion of sabotage surrounds
a bobsled crash that occurred during
a practice at Canada Olympic Park
yesterday. The sled's runners were
loosened to such an extent that one
flew off during the run. The driver,*

Olympic contender James Ramsey, was unable to control the severe fishtailing motion during a difficult turn. The sled flipped, dragging Ramsey and brakeman Quentin Porley with it for more than fifty meters on the track. Ramsey sustained a wrist injury in the accident that may prevent him from competing in the National trials and in the World Cup in Torino, Italy later this month.

Fellow bobsledder Joshua Gantz has been suspended from competition until the incident has been reviewed. No charges are pending at this time.

Josh crumpled the newspaper in his fist, clenching the wadded paper like he was trying to squeeze the words off the page.

"I figured you should know," I said. Nick and I had snuck away from the class to find Josh after Courtney told us he would be at Olympic Park today, trying to fix his sled.

"I guess I should have told that reporter my side of the story when I had the chance," Josh said. "Now look at the mess I'm in."

"Well, that guy who drove your sled didn't exactly go easy on you," Nick commented.

"I wouldn't expect him to. We're not exactly friends, and he knows I have a chance to beat him for a spot on the National team."

"Why did you lend him your sled, then?" I wanted to know.

Josh shrugged. "Trying to get along, I guess. To show I'm not out to get him." He gave a bitter laugh. "That sure backfired."

"Do you know how that runner got loose?" Nick asked.

"No idea," Josh answered, but he said it a little too quickly. "I'll leave it to the track officials to figure out."

"But—!" I began.

"Forget it." There was a hard edge to Josh's voice. "Thanks for letting me know about the article." He picked up his tools.

I frowned. "Listen, Josh. There's something else. Did anyone know that Ramsey was going to use your sled?"

Josh paused. "No, I offered it to him just

before practice. That's why he's so sure I loosened the runner."

"Did anyone else have access to your sled? Because I think maybe that sabotage was meant for you."

Josh's jaw tightened, and I knew immediately that this idea had already occurred to him. "Look, kid. I'm trying to be polite here, but back off, okay? You have no idea what you're talking about. Who says the sled was sabotaged in the first place? The runner could have just come loose."

"That much?" Nick sounded skeptical.

Josh rounded on him. "Yes, that much!"

Robyn stuck her head inside the bobsled shed. "You guys, hurry up! I told Mr. Kowalski you had to go to the bathroom fifteen minutes ago. We're supposed to be at the Ice House already."

"Okay. See ya around, Josh." I followed Nick outside. "I don't believe it," I said flatly. "I've never see a runner fly off a sled like that."

"And how many bobsled races have you actually witnessed?" Nick joked.

"It just doesn't seem likely," I said. "I think Josh is hiding something."

"Me too," Nick agreed. "What do you think, Robyn?"

No answer.

"Robyn?" I turned to see her crawling on her knees beside a garbage can outside the doorway of the shed. "What are you doing?"

"I saw something..." She reached into the crevice between the can and the shed wall and pulled out a tattered bit of paper.

"You're kneeling in the dirt just to pick up a piece of litter?" Nick said. "I know you're an enviro-nut, Robyn, but isn't this a little extreme?"

"It's a fifty-dollar bill!" Robyn was flushed with excitement.

"Really?" Nick dropped on all fours and began nosing around the can. "Maybe there's more. We could go out for pizza."

"Don't be dumb. We're not keeping it. Someone lost it. We should turn it in."

"Turn it in!" Nick looked at her like she had two heads. "It's dirty and ripped. It's probably been lost for ages. No one's going to claim it."

"Well, if they don't, I'll take you out for pizza," Robyn replied. "Come on. Let's go. Mr. Kowalski is probably looking for us." She pocketed the money and led the way to the Ice House, where bobsled and luge athletes practiced on an indoor track.

I glanced back at the long winding bobsled track. Canada Olympic Park was pretty big. I could see the ski jumps and the concrete tower at the top of the hill, the ski area and the big building that housed the Olympic Hall of Fame, the museum, the cafeteria and a bunch of other stuff. We could probably spend a month of field trips there and still not see everything.

Mr. Kowalski gave us a mildly annoyed look as we snuck into the back of the group. A young woman was standing at the front, demonstrating how to steer a practice bobsled. Robyn handed Mr. Kowalski the fifty-dollar bill with a quick, whispered explanation. I could see him nod; then he put the money in his wallet. I figured he would turn it in after the lecture. After we had toured the Ice House and taken some notes, we left for our lunch break.

The cafeteria and the Lost and Found were in the same building. Mr. Kowalski turned in the fifty-dollar bill, filled out a form so they could contact him if it wasn't claimed and shepherded our class into the cafeteria, which had enormous glass windows that looked out onto the ski hill. Some of the kids sat down right away and opened their lunch bags, but I got in line behind Mr. Kowalski. My lunch consisted of a withered pepperoni stick, a bag of soda crackers and an apple. My dad was picking up groceries tonight, but meanwhile I was starving. I wondered what I could get for two dollars and thirty-five cents, which was all the money I had.

While I was looking at the menu board, Mr. Kowalski ordered chocolate milk for the whole class. The gray-haired clerk hoisted a flat of milk containers onto the counter. Mr. Kowalski opened his wallet and handed her a very worn fifty-dollar bill.

The clerk took it and rang in the total, but as she moved to put it in the cash register drawer, she stopped. She glanced at the bill, and then she frowned and looked again. She moved sideways and carefully stepped on something on the floor. I thought maybe it was an alarm. I felt a sinking sensation in my stomach as I saw two burly security guards stride through the door.

"Is something the matter?" Mr. Kowalski asked.

"Yes, I'm afraid so." She caught the eye of the guards and nodded her head toward Mr. Kowalski. "We'll have to ask you to wait and answer a few questions for the police."

"The police!" Mr. Kowalski squawked. "Why?" The guards crept closer, ready to grab him if he should suddenly turn violent or try to flee.

"Because..." The clerk fixed him with a piercing stare. "The fifty-dollar bill you just gave me is counterfeit!"

chapter four

"Counterfeit!" Mr. Kowalski's jaw dropped. He looked at the fifty-dollar bill he had just given the cafeteria clerk. "I don't know anything about counterfeiting. I'm a junior high school teacher!"

"Well, you need to be more careful in your choice of second careers," the clerk scolded. "What are you teaching these kids? You should lead by example."

The buzz of voices rose behind us as the class realized what was going on.

"They're going to arrest Mr. Kowalski," someone whispered.

"But I'm not a counterfeiter!" Mr. Kowalski protested. Heads began to turn in our direction. "This is unbelievable."

"You've been caught with the evidence. I don't think that's so unbelievable," said the clerk.

Mr. Kowalski rubbed his temples. "You should stop watching those reality cop shows."

Several kids in our class snickered at that comment, just as two uniformed police officers entered the cafeteria, spotted us and strode over.

"We need to ask you a few questions."

"Aren't you going to read him his rights?" Robyn piped up. Most of our class fell silent, waiting to hear the answer.

Mr. Kowalski's mustache twitched. One of the officers frowned. "He's not under arrest," he told Robyn. "Yet," he added as Mr. Kowalski looked visibly relieved.

The other officer stepped forward. "We'll need you to come with us."

Mr. Kowalski nodded and turned to us. "Kids, I need you to go and finish your lunches. If I'm going to be more than a few minutes, I'll contact the school for another supervisor. Please stay together," Mr. Kowalski said. He looked at the officers. "Do you mind if we discuss this nearby? I don't want to leave the kids unattended."

The officer hesitated, and then he nodded. They led Mr. Kowalski to a table not far away. I followed slowly, finding a seat as close as possible. Robyn grabbed a chair beside me and motioned for Nick to join us. Nick plunked himself down in the chair opposite me. "What the heck is going on?" he whispered. "How did Kowalski end up with fake money?"

"Shhh!" Robyn stretched back in her chair, trying to eavesdrop.

"So, tell us where you might have picked up the bill," the younger officer was saying.

"I'm not part of a counterfeiting ring," Mr. Kowalski insisted.

"I'm sure you're not, sir," the officer said. "But we need to trace this bill. Can you tell me how long you might have had it, or where you might have gotten it?"

Mr. Kowalski shook his head. "I don't know."

"Do you spend a lot of cash?" the officer persisted.

"Not really. I usually use my debit card," Mr. Kowalski said.

"Can you think back to where you might have received a fifty-dollar bill? Returned merchandise, maybe?"

Robyn bolted upright. "A fifty-dollar bill? He paid with a fifty?"

I stared at her. "Yeah, so?"

"Was it dirty and ripped up?" she asked.

"Um...yeah. I think so. Why?" I said.

"Because," Robyn hissed, "that's probably the one I found outside by the shed. I bet Mr. Kowalski turned the wrong bill in to the Lost and Found."

"I hate to break this to you, Robyn," Nick said. "But people don't usually care if they get the exact bill back that they lost. It's the amount that matters."

"Nick, if you can't be helpful, you can just stay out of our investigation." Robyn shoved her chair back and marched over to the police.

"Our investigation?" I said. "Since when did this turn into our investigation?"

"Excuse me, officer," Robyn said. "But I have something to ask Mr. Kowalski."

"Yes, you can go to the bathroom," said the older officer impatiently.

"No, it's not that," she said.

The officer frowned. "We're trying to conduct an interview here."

"And I'm trying to help," Robyn said stubbornly. "I found a fifty-dollar bill outside, on the ground. I gave it to Mr. Kowalski to turn in to the Lost and Found. I think he gave them the wrong bill and paid the cafeteria with the fifty we found."

"Why do you think that?"

"The bill we found was torn and dirty. It looked like it had been outside for quite a while."

The policeman pulled the bill out of his pocket and glanced at it.

"That's definitely the one we found," said Robyn. "The corner got ripped off because it was snagged under the shed."

The officer stood up. "Can you show me where you found it?"

Robyn smiled. "Of course."

chapter five

"Hey, you guys, wait!" Courtney called as she tried to catch up. It was one of our last days at Canada Olympic Park, and Robyn, Nick and I were following Mr. Kowalski, along with the rest of the class. We were supposed to have a lesson with one of the curators about historical sports artifacts, but we were having trouble finding the right room.

"Maybe it's in the basement," Mr. Kowalski said, scratching his forehead. "Unless I have the wrong building altogether." He started off down the hallway, the rest of us trailing behind.

"Anything on Josh, yet?" Courtney whispered.

"Not so far," Robyn replied glumly.

"We're still working on it," Nick said.

We passed a number of closed doors. As Mr. Kowalski led us toward the stairs, Nick stepped on my flapping shoelace, nearly ripping it out of my shoe and sending me sprawling.

"Ow!" I complained, rubbing my elbow. I'd hit a doorknob on the way down.

"You okay?" Nick asked.

"Yeah." I picked myself up. The rest of the class was already clattering down the stairs, but Courtney and Robyn had stopped to watch me do the world's biggest face plant. I brushed off my jeans, trying to ignore the fact that you could toast marshmallows over the heat from my ears. Embarrassment always does that to me.

I'd knocked the door nearest me slightly open when I fell. I was about to reach out and close it, when a familiar voice floated through the crack. I had to strain to hear it over the clomping footsteps of my class.

"...forget about Josh. He's all taken care of," the voice said.

I froze. It was James Ramsey. I peeked through the crack and saw him, his back to the door, a telephone receiver pressed to his ear. I motioned frantically for Nick, Robyn and Courtney to come closer so they could hear.

"No, there's no one else who's even close to my race times," said Ramsey.

Pause.

Ramsey laughed. "Hah. I'll be on that track before you know it. The wrist's okay. I'll be ready to compete."

There was a longer pause this time.

"Yeah, but with Josh out, it leaves the National trials wide open for me. Winning has never been so easy."

Robyn gasped. "It sounds like he sabotaged the sled to get Josh out of the way." She inched the door open a little more. It squeaked softly.

"That's why...," Nick whispered and then froze as Ramsey turned and saw what must have looked like a row of eyeballs peering through the crack, "...we should RUN!" Nick yelled, grabbing Robyn's arm and hauling her to her feet. Ramsey had reached the door in two strides and threw it open.

"What are you kids doing?" Ramsey bellowed. The four of us were a scrambled knot of churning arms and legs. We bolted down the hall.

"Hey, come back here!" Ramsey shouted. He dropped the phone and chased us.

"Help!" Courtney squeaked. Fear spurred us on. We galloped to the stairwell and thundered down the stairs. Mr. Kowalski was nowhere to be seen.

"Where are they?" Robyn said frantically.

"This way." Nick pushed open the nearest door. Courtney, Robyn and I ran through the doorway, only to be stopped by a concrete wall.

"Where are we?" I said.

"In a storage room," Robyn said, pulling the door closed behind us. "Be really quiet."

We waited in the dim light. My heart hammered against my ribs and sweat trickled down my forehead, but outside everything was silent. Ramsey must have given up.

"I think it's safe," Courtney whispered. She shifted her backpack, and I heard the soft fluttering sound of paper hitting the floor.

"What's that?" I asked.

"I...uh...dropped something," Courtney said. I groped for a light switch and flicked it on. Blinking in the sudden brightness, I saw a bunch of money scattered on the floor of the closet. I saw twenty-dollar bills, a few fifties and some tens. Courtney tried to scoop them back into the envelope that had been in her backpack.

"Where did you get all that money?" Nick asked. His eyes narrowed.

"It's Josh's. I mean, it's for Josh." Courtney's face flushed bright red.

"Why would your brother let you carry around his money?" Robyn said. "My brother wouldn't let me carry his dirty laundry, let alone his life savings."

Courtney stuffed the last of the bills into the envelope without answering. She opened the door. "Come on, let's go, before Ramsey finds us."

"Too late." Nick swallowed hard.

James Ramsey stood in the doorway, a satisfied grin on his face.

chapter six

"So." James Ramsey advanced on us. We were trapped. Robyn, Nick and I cowered against the back wall of the storage room. Courtney gave a small whimper. "I want to know what you kids were doing back there." Ramsey glared at us.

"B-b-back where?" Courtney stammered.

"We didn't do anything. Trevor did a huge

face plant in the hall. We were just making sure he was okay, when you came blasting out of that office and scared the daylights out of us." Robyn spoke up defiantly.

I groaned to myself as Ramsey eyed me. There's nothing like having an Olympic-caliber athlete recognize you as a complete bozo. But Ramsey didn't seem to buy Robyn's explanation. After all, we *did* hear Ramsey telling someone on the phone that it was great that Josh had been suspended from competing. *And*, it sounded as though Ramsey had planned it.

Ramsey contemplated us, weighing what to do. Finally, he leaned so close I could smell the tuna fish on his breath. "If I find out that you three had anything to do with helping Josh Gantz sabotage that sled, there will be some serious trouble. Don't let me catch you snooping around here again, get it?" he said with soft menace.

My throat dry, I nodded with the others.

"Good. Get lost." Ramsey stood aside and pointed to the door.

We fled.

"I thought we weren't going to snoop around. Didn't we tell Ramsey that?" Nick whispered.

"He said not to let him catch us. So...we won't get caught," Robyn said. "Who has the flashlight?" The evening sky overhead was a dim purple. Canada Olympic Park was dark and quiet. Shadows blackened our path, but the ski hill blazed white under the electric lights. Night skiers swooped down the slope.

I handed Robyn the flashlight. I'd convinced my dad to drop us off tonight, with the excuse that we wanted to do more research for our field trip assignment. He was coming back for us when the park closed, which gave us about an hour to investigate. It must be easier to be a detective when you can drive.

"I still think it's a bad idea to be sneaking around here tonight," I said.

"Look, something's going on," Robyn pointed out. "If someone is sabotaging sleds, they're going to do it after hours, when no one is around. Plus, we found that counterfeit money right outside the shed. That's two reasons why we should be here."

"But why *tonight*?" I asked. The wind was icy, and it felt like snow was on the way. Another night would have been all right with me.

"Because tomorrow the National team officials are coming to tour the facility and see how the athletes are doing," Robyn said. "Courtney told me. It's a big deal to Josh, because he can't be there. It could hurt his chances at the trials."

"How do you figure that?" Nick said. "If Josh's time is faster than the other sleds, he makes the National team. It's that simple."

"Not quite," Robyn answered. "If there's a lot of publicity around the sabotage—and there has been already—do you really think people will want Josh representing Canada in front of the whole world? I say he ends up getting pulled, unless we can prove he didn't do it. And if he doesn't compete internationally, then his chances of making the Olympic trials someday are pretty slim."

Nick was silent, thinking that over.

"Someone's coming," I said. I heard the soft crunch of gravel behind us.

"Hide, quick!" Robyn whispered. She yanked Nick off the path, but the only thing handy to offer protection was a garbage can. It would hardly conceal three of us.

The crunching grew louder.

"Come on," I said. If it was James Ramsey, I definitely did not want to get caught twice. The Ice House was only about thirty feet away. Nick clicked the flashlight off and we ran quietly through the grass, flattening ourselves against the outside wall of the building.

"Move up, so we can see," Robyn said. She crouched down into the shadows and crawled forward, oblivious of the muddy ground. Two large figures emerged on the path. One of them had a sheet of paper in one hand. Was it Ramsey and his brakeman? I couldn't tell. They turned toward the Ice

House and walked directly toward us. I heard Robyn's quick intake of breath. Could they see us?

I got my answer.

"Someone's over there," one of them said.

"Run!" yelped Nick.

We tore away from the facility, clods of mud and damp leaves flying from our sneakers. Obviously Nick and I had the same idea—that if Ramsey got hold of us this time, we'd be in very big trouble.

"Which way?" gasped Robyn.

"Head for the parking lot. There'll be lots of people." My heart was hammering against my ribs. Nick sounded like a constipated buffalo, snorting and puffing. Robyn was ahead of both of us. She looked over her shoulder to make sure we were still with her and suddenly stopped. Nick and I nearly skidded into her.

"What's the matter?" I said.

"I don't think they're following us."

Sure enough, after a few seconds of jagged breathing, I could hear the quiet. There were no pounding footsteps, no yells, no big hairy guys with fists like sledgehammers.

"Maybe it wasn't Ramsey," I speculated.

"Well," Robyn said, looking somewhat ticked off. "We're going back, then."

"*What!*" Nick and I said.

"We have to see what's going on. We'll never find out who set up Josh at this rate." Robyn turned and headed back in the direction we just came from.

Nick looked at me and shrugged. "I guess it could have been maintenance people or something."

I took a deep breath and followed Robyn through the dark, Nick behind me. We caught up to Robyn and skirted the Ice House, sneaking closer from the other side.

Everything was quiet.

"I'm going in," Robyn said.

"Those guys could still be inside," I said.

"No, they're not. Look." Robyn pointed at the muddy footprints in the thin layer of snow. "They've left."

"How do you know those are their footprints?" I demanded, but it was too late. Robyn was already testing the door. It was unlocked.

"Come on," Robyn whispered. Nick and I slid through the door behind her.

The door shut with a soft thud. The indoor start tracks, where the bobsledders practice sprinting while they push the sleds, loomed ahead. They looked like big concrete slides under the eerie glow of a flickering fluorescent light.

I glanced around uneasily. Nick swallowed hard. But Robyn pointed to the muddy smudges on the floor. "Look," she whispered in triumph. "They might as well have signed their names!"

She followed the prints, which led directly to a bulletin board on the wall. "Check for clues. Anything to do with bobsledding, or Josh, or even Ramsey," she said.

I scanned the bulletin board. Among all the colored notices, a typewritten memo on white paper was pinned to the cork. I pulled it off and read it.

J.

The orange bananas are at the store.

They are a great so*ur*ce of zinC. I eXXpect you want s*o*me for lunch tomorrow. Bunches are avaiLable.

Us

I frowned at the message. Nick and Robyn peered over my shoulder to read.

"What does *that* mean?" Robyn asked, puzzled.

"Orange bananas?" Nick said. "Whoever heard of those?

"I don't know," I said. "But–!"

I heard the footstep too late. Someone grabbed my shoulder in a crushing grip.

"I'll take that!" a voice growled. The next instant, the message was ripped from my hand.

chapter seven

The hand on my shoulder tightened. I twisted
away and spun around, my fists raised.

"Josh!" Robyn gasped in relief. "What are
you doing here?"

"I was about to ask you the same thing."
Josh glanced at the note he'd just yanked out of
my hand. "Why are you kids sneaking around
the Ice House at this time of night?"

I stared at him. "That note was left for
you, wasn't it?"

"Why do you say that?" said Josh uneasily.

"It's addressed to 'J.' And it's funny that you just happened to be here."

Josh bristled. "I happened to be here because I'm an athlete who trains at this facility."

"An athlete who's suspended from training," I countered. "So why would you be hanging around here at night?"

Josh's face grew red. For a moment no one spoke. Robyn held her breath. Then Josh exhaled slowly. "Look, guys," he said, "you don't understand what's going on. You need to go home."

"We can't," Robyn said matter-of-factly. "Courtney asked us to investigate who framed you."

"My sister?" Josh closed his eyes. "Tell me this isn't happening. Tell me a bunch of kids are not playing detective with my life."

"She just wants to help, and so do we," Robyn retorted. "What makes you think we can't?"

Josh ignored that question. "You have to forget it. Forget you saw me here, forget the note, forget everything. I can handle my own problems."

"But what does the note mean? I never heard of orange bananas before," I persisted.

"Orange bananas?" Josh looked surprised.

"Yeah. See?" I showed him the note.

Josh hesitated. "Just some sports performance hocus-pocus. Health stuff, you know. It's not a big deal."

I didn't buy that explanation, but before I could argue, Josh steered us away from the bulletin board. "Look, I mean it. You have to stay away from here. He opened the door to the Ice House and peered into the darkness, and then he shut the door and faced us. "All right," he whispered. "I'm going. I want you guys to go up to the ski hill. There are a lot of people there. You catch your bus, or meet your parents or whatever you have to do, but get out of here. Okay?"

The desperate expression on Josh's face stopped all my arguments. Nick, Robyn and I exchanged glances, and slowly we all nodded.

"Good. And don't worry about me. I can take of myself." Josh smiled at us. "See you around." With that, he held open the door and ushered us out before disappearing into the dark.

The door shut behind us with a soft clunk. I looked at Robyn and Nick. "What's going on?" I said.

Nick shrugged. "No idea, but way more than Josh is telling."

"I think we should follow him," Robyn whispered. "Something is definitely up."

"Okay." I checked my watch. "Let's go. We'll lose him if we wait any longer."

We edged ourselves against the Ice House, in the shadows, and then we set off in the direction Josh had taken. A dim figure walked on the path ahead of us, heading toward the bobsled track.

"Is that Josh?" Robyn whispered.

"Shhh," Nick cautioned. He pointed up ahead. Two figures had joined the first one. They wore bulky jackets and toques. We watched as the three talked. Josh shook his head. One of the others gestured impatiently. Josh stepped back, but the figure moved closer, with one arm raised.

"This doesn't look good," Nick murmured.

"We have to do something," Robyn said anxiously.

I tried to think fast. The three of us might be able to rush one guy, but not two. If we ran for help, it would take time—too much time. I swallowed hard. I had another plan, but it wasn't great.

"Get ready to run," I whispered. "If they come after us, go for help as fast as you can."

"Trevor, what are you doing?" Robyn said in a panicked voice. But I ducked off the path and crept closer to the trio of men.

I cleared my throat as silently as possible, and then in a deep voice I barked out at the top of my lungs, "FREEZE! Police!"

The effect was immediate. All three men stood rooted to the spot for a fraction of a second. Then the other two took off running into the darkness beyond the bobsled track, while Josh stared at us when we emerged from the bushes. "What," he asked ominously, "are you doing here?"

"Saving your backside, apparently," Robyn retorted. "Who were those guys? How come they were threatening you?"

"Who says they were threatening me?" Josh answered.

"It's kind of obvious, Josh. When a guy raises his fist, he's not exactly getting ready to shake hands," Nick said.

Josh steered us toward the path that led to the parking lot. "Come on. This time I'll make sure you get to where you're supposed to go."

"You haven't answered the question," I reminded him.

"I'm not going to, either," Josh replied, an edge of anger in his voice. "I'm twenty years old, I'm in college and I don't have to answer to the junior high detective squad." He strode through the darkness, herding us ahead of him. Robyn, Nick and I were puffing by the time we reached the bottom of the ski hill, but Josh was hardly out of breath.

He turned to us, his jaw still clenched. "Listen," he hissed. "Stay away from here. I have better things to do than babysit the three of you." He walked away without a backward glance.

chapter eight

"Is it my imagination, or is Josh a little testy?" Robyn said at school the next morning.

"If you had those gorillas picking a fight with you, you'd be testy too." Nick snorted.

"So, what's the next move?" I asked.

Robyn pursed her lips thoughtfully. "Well, Josh wants us to stay away from Olympic Park, Ramsey wants us to stay away from Olympic Park. So, I say we go back there as soon as possible."

I decided to ignore that suggestion. "Do you really think that Ramsey would want Josh off the National team so badly he would stage the sabotage and then threaten him?"

"Well, it sure sounded that way when Ramsey was on the phone," Nick said. "But we don't know if Ramsey was one of the guys hassling Josh last night or not. There were two of them."

"The second guy could have been Ramsey's brakeman." Robyn yanked on her lock. She tugged, rewound the combination and tugged again, but it refused to open. "I hate this locker." Robyn dealt the metal door a vicious kick. "It never works."

"Try it again. You're gonna be late," Nick said.

Robyn spun the combination slower this time. When it clicked open Robyn breathed a sigh of relief. "Finally." She stowed her backpack inside and rummaged around for her books. "Courtney is organizationally challenged," she said from the depths of her locker. "I can never find anything."

"Maybe you should switch lockers," I suggested.

"I wish." Robyn held up an assortment of papers. "Like, what is this stuff? The J. G. Foundation Raffle, ticket stubs, homework, late slips, why is it all crammed in here? I can't even find my sneakers." She stopped, suddenly very still. "You guys?" she said.

"Yeah?" Nick exchanged glances with me.

Robyn pulled her head out of the locker, her eyes wide. "There's an ice pick in my locker."

"So?" Nick said.

"So, who put it in here?" said Robyn.

Nick shrugged. "Courtney, I guess."

"But why would she do that?" asked Robyn.

"I dunno," Nick said. "It's not exactly a crime to own an ice pick."

"Nick, an ice pick is a *weapon*!" Robyn hissed. She held the handle of the pick gingerly, the wicked-looking metal spike protruding from her fingers.

"No, it isn't. It's a tool. Courtney probably had some of Josh's bobsled stuff in her backpack and it fell out. That would make sense," said Nick.

"Yeah, it would, if bobsledders used ice picks, which they don't," Robyn retorted. "Besides, there's a note on it." She hesitated. "Should we read it?"

Nick groaned. "Robyn! We're supposed to be investigating, remember?"

"Oh right." Robyn plucked the note off the handle and unfolded it. "J. Meeting's off for lunch. Need bananas tomorrow night, 9 PM, or *you'll* be on ice. Us." She stared at us, wide-eyed. "It's from the same guys as the last note."

"Yeah, but except for the banana thing, this one makes sense," I said. "The last one was full of typos."

"Maybe they were just in a hurry with that one," Nick suggested.

"I don't think so," I said slowly. "I wish we could get a look at that note again."

"You mean, this note?" Robyn said, rummaging through the tattered duffel bag at the bottom of the locker. "Nick was right about one thing: this stuff is Josh's."

She poked her head out of the locker and handed me the note. "I wonder why Courtney has it in here."

"Lots of reasons," Nick said. "Maybe he forgot the bag, and Courtney brought it so she could give it to him later."

"Or maybe she just took it," Robyn retorted.

"Maybe she did," Nick countered. "She's worried about him. She could have found the notes and brought them to school for *us* to look at."

"True," Robyn admitted. "But what if she's involved somehow? That wad of money she dropped seems a little suspicious, if you ask me. What if the ice pick is hers?"

"With a note taped to it that threatens her brother?" Nick snorted. "I doubt she'd bring that to school."

"Quit it, you guys," I said. I unfolded the paper. It was the message we'd found on the bulletin board at the Ice House last night. "You see?" I said. "This is just weird." I held out the note so the others could see.

J.

The orange bananas are at the sto*re*.
They are a great so*ur*ce of zinC. We
eXXpect some f*o*r lunch tomorrow.
Bunches are avaiLable.

Us

"Who's the 'J'?" I asked. "We've been
assuming it's Josh, but what if it's Ramsey?
His first name is James, remember?"

Robyn's eyes widened. "That's right! But
Josh was in the Ice House when we found
it."

"He could have been waiting for Ramsey
to pick up the note. Maybe Josh knows
what's going on, and that's why his sled was
sabotaged. It could be a warning to keep quiet
about what he knows," Nick speculated.

My head was spinning. "Are you saying
there's another reason the sled was wrecked that
doesn't have to do with the National trials?"

"Maybe. I'm just saying we shouldn't rule
it out."

"Let's focus on the notes," Robyn suggested.
"Maybe they'll give us some clues."

"Okay. So why would the C in zinc and the L in available be capitalized?" I said. "Or the X's in expect? And why are there two?"

"Somebody doesn't know how to spell?" Nick suggested.

"Maybe, but doesn't that seem like a strange mistake?" Robyn said. "I think Trevor's right. Maybe it's a code."

"Josh said it was a health food thing." Nick peered over my shoulder at the note.

"And you really believe that?" Robyn said. "Orange bananas don't exist."

Nick dumped out his lunch bag and unearthed a partly squashed banana. "Okay, so what else could the message mean?"

Robyn took the banana and turned it over in her hand. "Well, since we're talking about Josh, if you look at the banana like this, it looks like a bobsled."

"Yeah, and Josh's sled is orange!" I said. "I bet that's it!"

Nick groaned. "That's way too obvious."

"Yeah, but it makes sense," I argued. "You said that maybe Josh is being warned to keep quiet. What if this note is a coded message about more sabotage to his bobsled!"

"But Josh isn't even allowed to practice right now," Robyn protested.

"Exactly!" I said. "So if someone is trying to scare him, now's a good time to let him know that when he gets back on the track, things could get ugly."

Nick nodded. "Seems logical to me."

"What if the note was left for James Ramsey, not Josh?" Robyn said.

I paused, thinking. "Well, Ramsey could be getting instructions for more sabotage to Josh's sled. If Josh figured it out and was waiting last night to catch Ramsey in the act, that would clear Josh's name and put Ramsey out of the competition."

The three of us stared at each other. We had two very plausible explanations for that note, but no proof.

I tucked the notes inside the pocket of my jeans. "I think it's time we followed James Ramsey for a while."

chapter nine

"How many times am I going to freeze my butt off on this hill?" Nick complained, shifting his snow-crusted sneakers to thaw his feet. The wind was whistling down the hillside. I looked up at the winding empty bobsled track and the rolling expanse of bracken that stretched on either side. Snow was already gathering in the clumps of grass.

"It won't be long now," I answered. I checked my watch. Ramsey hadn't been in the coach's office or the Ice House. Practice would be starting soon.

"I don't understand what we're going to learn by watching Ramsey practice," Robyn complained.

"We're not going to watch him practice. We're going to wait until we know he's practicing, and then we're going to search his car," I said.

"We're going to what!" Robyn squeaked.

"Search the car. We'd better go down to where the athletes park. We need to see which car is his." I started down the path.

"Tell me we're not going to break in if he locks it," Nick said.

"No, but we will look in the windows and see if there's anything to prove that Ramsey had something to do with the coded notes or sabotaging the bobsled. Then we'll go to the police."

"Not the coach?" Robyn asked.

"Nope. For all we know, the coach is the one who planned the sabotage in the first place, and Ramsey is his right-hand man. They could have set up Josh to take the fall. Maybe the coach wants Ramsey on the National team, and Josh is a threat."

Robyn stared at me, her mouth agape. "You don't really believe that, do you?"

"No, but it's a possibility. We have to go to the police as soon as we find some evidence. We don't know who to trust."

"This is getting way too complicated," said Nick.

We passed a couple of guys dressed in maintenance overalls, carrying toolboxes, near the bobsled shed. I bumped into one by accident, and he looked as startled as I felt. The toolbox crashed to the ground, spilling several tools into the snow.

"Sorry," I muttered, hoping Ramsey wouldn't pick this moment to show up. I scooped up the screwdrivers, brushed the snow off the handles and gave them back.

The man waved me off. "No problem," he said. His voice was thick with an accent I couldn't place.

"Practice must be starting," said Robyn. "They've opened the shed."

I glanced at my watch again. "Not for another ten minutes. Robyn, you hide outside and watch for Ramsey's car. Nick and I are going to have a quick look."

"We are?" Nick swallowed. The shed, as big as it was, was just an open room with one door. There was no place to hide if Ramsey appeared.

"Come on." I yanked Nick through the open shed door. It was dim inside. Rows of bobsleds were stored in compartments that were screened with gates made of chain-link fence. Most of the gates were padlocked. Only one swung open gently.

"Ramsey's sled is red," Nick whispered. "I think it's over here."

We peered through the chain-link gate. The red bobsled gleamed softly, its rounded front facing us. There was an open toolbox nearby on the floor. Allen wrenches and a few other tools were in the top tray.

"Do you see anything?" Nick whispered.

"Not yet." I got down on my hands and

knees. And then I spotted it. A smaller version of the ice pick we'd found in Robyn's locker had rolled underneath Ramsey's sled. I nudged Nick. "Look," I said.

"It's the same," he whispered. "That ice pick has the same black handle with a red band around the top."

"That's what I thought," I said. "They're probably from the same set."

"Which means...?"

"Which means we have to get it," I said with determination. "This could be the proof we need."

"How? The gate's locked."

"I think I can reach it if I can get my arm underneath the fence," I said. I lay flat on the concrete and stretched my arm through the gap between the floor and the gate. Farther...a little farther...I grasped the ice pick with two fingers and drew it out.

"Trevor, someone's coming!" Nick whispered. The crunch of footsteps on the gravel was getting louder.

I tried to slide my arm out, but the

sleeve of my jacket caught on the wire of the fence.

"Come on!" Nick urged.

I worked the fabric free and, keeping a careful hold of the ice pick, yanked my arm out. I could hear voices now, deep male voices.

"It's Ramsey," I whispered.

"He'll pulverize us if he catches us." Panic showed on Nick's face.

I scanned the room. There was no place to hide, and we couldn't escape without being seen. My eyes lighted on the one unlocked gate. "Quick, in here."

I edged through the gate, praying that it wouldn't squeak. Nick and I scrambled into the orange bobsled inside the cubicle. This was Josh's sled.

"Duck down!" I leaned forward in the sled, with my head between my knees. The seconds ticked by. I began to get a cramp in my leg, and I wondered how the bobsledders could hold this position while they were rocketing down the track at ten hundred miles an hour.

I couldn't hear the voices anymore. I chanced a glance upward, and that's when I saw it.

One of the cables that steered the driving mechanism of the sled was cut halfway through. And taped to it was a note, written in red ink.

There was just one word on the note:

Reconsider.

chapter ten

"That's terrible," Robyn said, a horrified look on her face. "If Josh used that sled and didn't find the note, the cable would break while he's driving."

Courtney stepped up to the locker and overheard Robyn. "What cable?" she asked suspiciously.

I hesitated. "One of the driving cables on Josh's sled. Nick and I found it severed with another note."

Courtney's eyes widened. "He would have crashed for sure. He could have been killed!"

"I know," I said. I showed Courtney the ice pick I'd taken from Canada Olympic Park.

"This looks like the same one I found inside Josh's sports bag!" Courtney gasped. "Where did you get this?"

"We found it under Ramsey's bobsled. If it's Ramsey's, it would link him to the threats."

"But we need to prove it," Nick added. "I have a mini-fingerprinting kit I got for my birthday when I was eight. We could dust for prints."

Robyn shot him a withering stare, but I nodded. "That's not a bad idea. We might need that."

"I want to know why you had that sports bag to begin with," Robyn interrogated Courtney.

Courtney frowned. "Why, for you guys, of course. I found the ice pick and the notes, and I thought you should see them. Why else would I bring it?"

Robyn weighed Courtney's response. "Okay," she said at last, nodding. She turned to me. "What do you think that last note meant by 'Reconsider'?" she asked.

I shrugged. "If I had to guess, I'd say Josh has said no to something, and whoever is making the threats is trying to get him to change his mind."

"So we should talk to Josh," Robyn said slowly.

Nick shook his head. "Do you really think Josh is going to spill his guts to us? No, Robyn. We have to figure out those notes. Someone is threatening Josh, and the stakes are getting higher. If we want to help him, we have to break that code."

"Good luck," Robyn said without enthusiasm.

"Well, we know they mean Josh's bobsled when they talk about orange bananas. Nothing else seems to have a hidden meaning," I said. I opened the first note with the coded message and read it again.

J.

The orange bananas are at the stor*e*. They are a great so*ur*ce of zinC. We eXXpect some f*o*r lunch tomorrow. Bunches are avaiLable.

Us

"Let's concentrate on the letters that stand out," I suggested.

Nick read the note over my shoulder. "What about the words with the underlined letters? Store, source and for. Go to the source for the store?"

"No, what does that have to do with a bobsled?" Robyn snorted. "It doesn't even make sense."

"Well, then you try, genius," I answered.

"What about taking the underlined letters out and putting them together?" Robyn said. "*E*, *ur* and *o*. What does that spell?"

"Euro," Nick said. "That's the money in Europe, kind of like our dollar."

"Money?" I could see the light dawning in Robyn's eyes. I was thinking the same thing. "That's kind of a coincidence," I said.

"Considering we found counterfeit money under the bobsled shed at Canada Olympic Park."

"It's no coincidence," Robyn said tersely. "Keep going. What do the capital letters mean?"

I stared at the note. *ZinC, eXXpect* and *avaiLable*. The words themselves didn't seem to mean anything. Maybe the letters did, but they didn't spell anything. "Someone wanted those letters to be really visible," I said. "What could *C, XX* and *L* stand for?" I asked.

Robyn was thinking. "Is there some symbol for money? Like when you put *X*'s and *O*'s at the end of a letter for hugs and kisses?"

Nick rolled his eyes. "I doubt we're talking about hugs and kisses, Robyn. Someone's threatening Josh with an ice pick, remember?"

"I know that." Robyn blushed. "I just mean, is there a symbol for money, like fifty-dollar bills, or something."

"Fifty dollars? Why fifty?" Nick asked.

"Because we found a counterfeit fifty-dollar bill, doofus!" Robyn said.

But Nick wasn't paying attention. "Let me see that note," he demanded. I handed it over. "You know, Robyn has a point. *XX* is the Roman numeral for twenty. *C* is the numeral for one hundred. And *L* stands for fifty. They could be talking about twenty- fifty- and one-hundred-dollar bills."

"Not dollars," I reminded him. "Euros."

"Euros? Why Euros? They wouldn't be any good here," Nick said.

"No, but the World's competition is in Italy!" Robyn nearly shouted in excitement. People turned to stare. She dropped her voice to a whisper. "They're counterfeiting Euros, and how much do you want to bet they want Josh to get the money over to Italy inside his bobsled? That explains everything. They keep trying to get Josh to cooperate, because who would ever think to look inside a bobsled?"

"But what have they got on him? Why would they even think Josh would do it?" I argued.

"Maybe they offered him money," Robyn suggested.

Courtney, who had been listening silently

the whole time, suddenly made a strangled noise.

Nick shot her a wary look. "How about all the cash Courtney dropped out of her backpack when we were hiding from Ramsey in that broom closet? She said that money was for Josh."

"That's right, you did," I said, watching Courtney's face go from a tired, pasty white to bright red. "Do you know something about this that you're not telling us?"

"No," Courtney squeaked.

"For that matter," Nick continued. "Maybe Courtney and Josh were working together to make it seem like James Ramsey is up to no good, when they were part of a counterfeiting ring!"

"No, we weren't! I mean it!" Courtney's eyes filled with tears. "Why would I ask you guys for help, if it meant you might find out I was some kind of crook?"

"That's true," I said.

"It's just that, Josh *does* need money," Courtney went on. "He wants to buy specialized sled runners from Germany.

He thinks they'll help him in the National trials, but they're really expensive."

"Isn't that, like, cheating?" Robyn asked.

"No!" Courtney's temper flared. "Josh wouldn't cheat. You can use different kinds of runners as long as they meet the Canadian standards."

"So, where'd all that money come from that you had in your backpack?" Nick wanted to know.

Courtney looked down at her feet. "Well, I was trying to help Josh, so I kind of made up, um...this raffle, to collect money."

"You made up a *what*?" Nick said.

"Is that what the J. G. Foundation is... the Josh Gantz Foundation? And all those tickets in our locker?" Robyn exclaimed in horror. "You were going to steal money from all those people?"

"No!" Courtney said desperately. "I wasn't stealing anything. I was going to buy a TV for the prize, but I didn't know how much they were! Now I don't even have enough tickets sold to buy the prize, let alone help Josh."

"You have to give that money back, Courtney," I said.

"I know." Courtney gulped. "I will."

"If you don't," Nick's eyes narrowed, "we'll tell the police. What you're doing is fraud."

"I will, I swear." Courtney held her hands up in surrender. "I'll go door-to-door to every house and explain."

"And," I added, "the note tells Josh to meet them tonight. We need to talk to Josh again. This time, we need some answers."

chapter eleven

"Coach, come on. It's been a week now. There's absolutely no proof that I did anything to that sled. You've got to let me back on the track."

I glanced at Nick and Robyn. We were back at Canada Olympic Park, walking toward the storage shed for the bobsleds, when we heard Josh's voice.

"Josh, we're still checking into it. It would look bad if..."

"I don't care if it looks bad!" Josh interrupted. "I've trained for four years for this, and I'm not missing the National trials because of some accident that I had nothing to do with."

The coach paused. "I understand how you feel, but until I get the official okay, I'm not supposed to let you anywhere the track."

"Coach, please! I have to practice. I'm going to lose everything I've worked for if I can't keep training." Josh sounded desperate.

The coach sighed. "I can't. You know I can't. But don't worry so much. Keep up the weight training, work on your sprints and you'll be okay. Your brakeman has been out here practicing with Ramsey, so he'll still be ready to go when you're back."

"Ramsey?" The bitterness in Josh's voice was obvious. "Why?"

"Well, he's fast," the coach said reluctantly. "If you aren't allowed to compete..."

"Then he'll just jump ship and race with Ramsey, is that it?" Josh said. "Well, that's just great!" He stomped away, rounding the corner of the building and nearly plowing right into us.

"You again!" he complained. "I don't need you guys on top of everything else."

"Josh, I know this is a bad time, but we really need to talk to you," I said.

"It's important," Robyn added.

"It's about the orange bananas," Nick said.

Josh ran a hand through his hair, making it stick out in all directions. "You're right, this is a bad time," he snapped. He walked away from the shed.

Since he hadn't actually told us to get lost, we followed him. Courtney hadn't come with us—she was returning the raffle money to its rightful owners.

Josh headed toward his car, glanced back and saw us trailing him. He sighed and folded his arms across his chest. "Okay. What's up?" He leaned against the fender of his battered Plymouth.

Robyn pulled the ice pick out of her backpack. "Have you seen this before?"

Josh's face lost some color. "Where did you get that?" he asked.

"So you do recognize it, then. What about the note?" Robyn persisted.

Josh grabbed the ice pick. "How did you get this?" he demanded.

"Courtney found it in your bag after you came home from the track last night. She's worried about you, and so are we. What's going on, Josh?" I said.

"Nothing. And anyway, I can handle this without the junior high detective squad."

"Can you?" Robyn challenged. "I'm not so sure. We just heard you begging your coach to let you get back to training. You haven't managed to find out who sabotaged your sled, or why, and you haven't done anything to clear your name so you can go to the National trials. Almost everyone but us believes you're guilty. And I can tell you, if you don't do something to change that, you can kiss the National team good-bye!"

Josh frowned.

"Everything you've worked for—gone." Robyn pressed the point home. "No World's competition, no Europa Cup and definitely no Olympics. Is that what you want?"

Josh remained silent.

"Maybe you should let us help, Josh," Nick said. "We've already figured out a lot."

"You're just kids. Keep out of it." Josh gritted his teeth.

"We can't," Robyn said. "We've already found the counterfeit money and turned it in."

"What?!" said Josh, his face revealing total panic.

"Ah-HAH!" said Robyn, stabbing her finger at Josh's chest. " I knew you knew about the money."

Josh looked away, a red flush burning his cheeks. "I don't know much," he admitted finally. "These two guys offered to help me win the National trials. I thought at first they would help me get the specialized runners I want for the sled, so I listened to what they had to say.

"They left a voice mail for me to pick up that weird note in the Ice House—the one you guys found. Then they offered me money to use my sled to transport a package to Italy—if I won. That sounded fishy enough, but they also hinted that they would take care of my competition at the trials to make sure I would qualify. I didn't know exactly what they had in mind, but I'd heard enough at that point and I said I wasn't interested. I figured that would be the end of it." Shaking his head, Josh continued. "But it wasn't. They started threatening me—said I'd be sorry if I didn't help them. I told them to take a hike. I don't know if they're scared I'll go to the police, but they just won't leave me alone."

"I'd say you're the one they're trying to scare," commented Robyn. "After leaving you an ice pick as a present."

Josh gave us a wry grin. "Yeah, maybe. But I was just going to ignore it. What can they do?"

"Maybe a lot," Nick said ominously. "Did you know about the counterfeiting?"

Josh shook his head. "I suspected, but I didn't know for sure. They dropped hints about the package in the bobsled. How did you figure it out?"

"We decoded the message that was left at the ice house. These guys aren't fooling around," I answered.

"You mean the note that was full of typos about the orange bananas? You've got to be kidding," Josh answered.

"They aren't typos, they're clues. We think the note meant they want you to transport twenty, fifty and one hundred Euro bundles inside your bobsled to the World's competition in Italy," I said.

"How was I supposed to know what that dumb note meant?" Josh snorted.

Robyn smothered a smile. "Was Ramsey ever part of it?"

"No." Josh shook his head. "Not that I know about, anyway."

Robyn and I glanced at each other. If the counterfeiters were behind all the threats, how had Ramsey ended up with an identical ice pick under his bobsled?

Nick speculated out loud. "So they decided to send the ice pick and scare you into meeting with them tonight."

"Well, I'm not going to." Josh frowned.

"They can't force me to do anything, and I can always go to the police."

"I don't think you want to do that," Nick said.

"We don't really have any proof," Robyn explained. "The police might look at these notes, but there's no way to prove the counterfeiters sent them. It could be anybody. Ramsey, for one."

"But," I said, "if you go, and we stake out the meeting place, we'll get the proof we need. *Then* we can go to the police."

"No." Josh was adamant. "I can't let you do that. It's too dangerous. I'll go."

"You might need help," Robyn protested.

"I can deal with it." It was his turn to point at Robyn. "You kids forget this conversation ever happened. I already told you, I don't need to babysit you guys, so stay home where you belong!"

chapter twelve

"Ouch!" Nick yelped. "Get off my foot, Robyn!"

"Get down!" I whispered. "They might be coming."

The three of us settled into our very cold, uncomfortable positions near the finish line of the bobsled track. The early winter darkness had settled all around us, broken only by the glow of light on the platform at the end of the track.

"If I had a buck for every time I've been freezing my butt off in the bushes at Olympic Park, I could afford a vacation in Hawaii," Nick grumbled, massaging his toe through his snow-encrusted sneaker.

"Shhh," Robyn hissed. "Trevor, have you got the coach's phone number?"

"You've asked me about six times. Yeah, I've got it."

"The cell phone? With batteries, this time?" she continued.

"Yeah, I have the phone, and it's charged," I answered. Robyn was never going to let me forget the time the three of us got locked in the museum and our cell phone was dead.

Alone, Josh leaned against a stair railing on the concrete platform, just within our line of sight.

"Okay," Nick said. "So, when the counterfeiters show up, we sneak closer. When they're talking to Josh, we video the whole thing. Then we phone the coach, show him the footage and call the cops."

"I think we should phone the coach and let him listen to Josh and the counterfeiters over the phone. Then we would have another witness," Robyn said.

"We could do that," I said. "It might help, especially if the sound quality on the video isn't great." I glanced around, worried. "The wind is really blowing. Usually wind makes a lot of noise on a tape. We're going to have to get really close to record the conversation."

"Great," Nick said without enthusiasm.

"I think someone's coming," Robyn whispered.

Two men emerged from the darkness and approached Josh on the platform.

"This is it," Robyn said. She began dialing the coach's number.

"Get ready to move closer," I commanded.

"I've got his answering machine," Robyn said.

"Just tell him who we are, that we're at Olympic Park and that Josh is in trouble. Then leave the line open. Hopefully the machine will run long enough to record something," I answered. We crept toward the platform, Robyn clutching the cell phone in her fist. My sneakers slid on the icy mud as we crouched down.

The two men had their backs to us. Nick slowly raised the video camera over the edge of the platform.

"I'm not really prepared to lend my sled, without knowing what's going on," Josh said.

One of the men turned. I could see the deep scowl on his face. I'd seen him before, but it took me a minute to place him. He was the guy I'd bumped into outside the storage shed the day we found the ice pick under Ramsey's sled.

"We can't give you any more details," he said in the same thick accent. "We only need to put packages inside the sled to get them to Italy."

"Packages of fake euros?" Josh asked.

The men glanced at each other. At that moment, my foot slipped. I bumped into Nick, and the handle of the video camera made a scraping noise against the platform.

The two men looked over. They'd seen us *and* the camera.

"You set us up!" one of them growled. He grabbed Josh roughly and punched him hard in the gut. Josh doubled over with a sick-sounding wheeze. "Get those kids!" the counterfeiter shouted to his partner.

Robyn gave a short shriek and flung the only weapon she had—the cell phone—as hard as she could at our attacker's face. For once she hit her target and nailed him right in the forehead. It stunned him long enough for Nick to get a better grip on the camera and skid away from the platform.

"Run!" I shouted. We careered down the short slope to the road. The darkness swallowed us. I listened, but I couldn't hear footsteps behind us.

"Where are we going?" Robyn gasped as I yanked her sideways.

"We need help. Fast. We can't leave Josh. There's a light in the Ice House. Maybe someone's there. If not, Nick and I will go back. Robyn, you'll have to find a phone, and call nine-one-one."

"Okay!" Robyn gulped.

I tried the door; it was unlocked. We rushed inside. There was only one person in the Ice House, examining a pair of bashed-up runners.

James Ramsey.

chapter thirteen

I felt like I'd swallowed an icicle. Of all the people who might help Josh, Ramsey was the last person on the list.

He glared at us, suspicion etched in every line of his face. "What are you doing here?" Ramsey snarled. "Checking to see how your latest sabotage attempt turned out?" He held the bashed-up bobsled runners in one fist. "You kids and Josh make quite a team."

"It wasn't us!" Robyn's voice sounded shrill with panic.

"Yeah, sure," Ramsey answered.

"How bad is the damage?" I asked. "Are your runners totally wrecked?"

Ramsey glanced at them in disgust. "They aren't mine. *Someone*," he eyed us, "left them in my bag."

But something clicked inside my brain. We knew Josh hadn't sabotaged his own sled. On the other hand, it was unlikely Ramsey would sabotage it, knowing he was driving it during practice and could get injured. What if someone else had loosened those runners? Someone who wouldn't be using the bobsled? Someone who was pressuring Josh to do what he—or rather they—wanted?

The counterfeiters. It had to be. They wouldn't have guessed Josh would get suspended, and now Ramsey had a pair of ruined runners left with his equipment. If those runners were from Josh's sled...It reeked of a set-up. The counterfeiters needed to get Josh back in competition, so they were going to frame Ramsey with a second sabotage attempt.

I remembered the tools spilling into the snow the day I bumped into the counterfeiter—I was sure some of them had red-rimmed, black handles. What if they had planted the ice pick under Ramsey's sled to make it look like he had been threatening Josh?

In that second, I decided to trust Ramsey.

"Look, we need your help," I said. "We need a phone. Josh is up at the bobsled track, getting the snot kicked out of him by a couple of guys from a counterfeiting ring."

Nick and Robyn looked at me like I was crazy, but they weren't the only ones.

"*What*?" Ramsey said.

"They're crooks. They've been trying to get Josh to use his sled to transport fake Euros to Italy. They sabotaged Josh's bobsled, and now they've set you up with these runners, to get you to take the blame."

I could see the recognition dawn on Ramsey's face. "Yeah, that makes some sense. There's been some pretty weird stuff going on. You said Josh is up at the track right now?"

"Yes, at the finish line. He might be hurt," Robyn said in a scared voice. "They punched him really hard."

"Robyn whacked one of them in the head with the cell phone, so now we have no way to call the police," Nick added.

Ramsey's jaw tightened. "Phone's over there." He gestured toward the wall. Robyn ran to make the call to 9-1-1. "Let's get going. Show me where he is."

The three of us raced for the door. Within a few seconds, Robyn joined us.

"I told the dispatcher what was going on. I think she thinks I'm crazy," Robyn said.

The blackness outside closed around us like a giant fist. Ramsey led the way, and within minutes I saw the platform ahead of us. Josh knelt in a crumpled heap on the deck, while one of counterfeiters yelled at the other.

"What do you mean, you let those kids get away? They have us on videotape, you doorknob! The police will recognize us. We have to find them and get that camera!"

"I don't think so!" Ramsey replied. He jumped on the platform and shoved one guy roughly to the floor. The other counterfeiter rushed him. Ramsey managed to land a punch just as the first counterfeiter grabbed him from behind.

"Hey!" I yelled from the shadows. It was instinctive and stupid. The counterfeiters turned and saw us.

"Get them, quick!" shouted the first counterfeiter, wrestling with Ramsey.

The second counterfeiter lunged for us. Robyn squeaked and Nick dodged. We ran for the blackness that surrounded the bobsled track.

Panic spurred us on. I doubt an Olympic runner could have caught us in those first few seconds. We hit the path that led up the bobsled track and sprinted.

"Trevor, he's going to catch us!" Robyn panted. "There's no place to go. We can't run all the way to the top!"

"We don't have to," I said. "The ski hill runs alongside it. We just have to make it there."

Robyn looked at the stretch of bushes and undulating grass that disappeared into the darkened ridge. "You're kidding," she said in disbelief.

"Isn't there a fence?" Nick puffed.

"Not everywhere. Watch for a break in it when we get close," I replied. I could hear the pounding of footsteps behind us. I grabbed Robyn's elbow and put on a burst of speed. "Hurry!"

We ran in silence, but after a few minutes Nick was breathing hard and Robyn was beginning to slow down. My own breath caught painfully in my side.

"Just a bit farther, guys," I gasped. "It's not far..."

"But far enough." The second counterfeiter stepped out of the shadows just ahead of us on the path. Somehow, he'd managed to get ahead of us. We froze in mid-stride.

"Give me the video camera," the counterfeiter said. He didn't look like a crook. He was about twenty-five with blond hair and glasses.

"I can't," Nick said. "My dad will kill me."

"And you think I won't? That's very trusting of you," the counterfeiter said with soft menace. "What I really want is the tape. Hand it over."

"What about Josh?" I said.

"Josh knows more than he should. If he won't work with us, he'll have to be persuaded to keep his mouth shut."

I didn't like the sound of that. I exchanged glances with Robyn and Nick.

"Give me the tape," the counterfeiter demanded.

I put my hand slowly into my jacket pocket where I'd stashed an extra tape for the stakeout and held it out to him.

"Nice try," the counterfeiter said. "Now give me the one in the camera." He reached out to grab Nick.

As though we had planned it all along, Nick stretched backward, holding the camera over the bobsled track. When the counterfeiter reached for it, Robyn and I shoved him as hard as we could. He somersaulted into the track.

"You rotten, little—!" he sputtered, swearing as he tried to clamber out. His shoes slipped and slid on the ice. For a moment, he looked like he was running in place, before he lost his balance and did a face plant on the ice.

The counterfeiter glared at us, and then he tried to slowly maneuver himself to the edge. He made it a few inches, but then his feet went straight out from under him and he landed hard on his backside.

"See you at the bottom," I called back. We started toward the ski hill, but a loud vibration suddenly started on the track. For the second time, we froze.

Whum-whum-whum-whum-whum.

"It's a sled!" Robyn cried. "Someone's coming down the track!"

The counterfeiter's face turned white. "Help me! Please!"

"Trevor, if he gets hit by a sled, it could kill him!" Robyn said.

I knew that. My stomach twisted and I bit my tongue to keep down the nausea. If we saved him, he could hurt us. If we didn't...

Whum-whum-whum-whum-whum.

I ran to the edge of the track and reached out my hand. He grabbed it and tried to stand up, but even holding on to me, his feet couldn't grip. He slid down the track, almost dragging me with him. "Nick, help me!" I yelled.

Nick grabbed the man's other arm, and we leaned back and pulled.

Whum-whum-whum-whum-whum.

"Hurry!" Robyn yelled. She grasped the man's jacket and yanked. He managed to get one leg up on the side of the wall. He tumbled down and landed with a crash on the ground.

WHUM-WHUM-WHUM-WHUM-WHUM!

Dazed, the man looked up. Instead of a sled rocketing down the track, a helicopter crested the ridge of the hill. A brilliant searchlight blinded everyone, and a voice boomed over the helicopter's bullhorn.

"Police! Don't move!"

chapter fourteen

Ignoring the warning, the counterfeiter scrambled to his feet and took off into the bush. The helicopter trained its searchlight on him, leaving us breathless in the dark.

"Where does he think he's going?" Robyn wondered. "The helicopter will track him no matter where he hides."

"Not if he can lose them in that heavy bush," Nick said grimly.

"They can't arrest him from that thing," I said. "They must be sending officers on foot."

Sure enough, within a few minutes, two uniformed officers arrived, puffing from the run uphill. The officer took one look at the terrain and groaned.

His partner watched the searchlight and said, "He's backtracking."

"Radio for K-nine," commanded the first officer. "And get these kids out of here!" He took off into the darkness after the counterfeiter.

"Let's go!" the second officer said to us. He made us jog a good clip down the path, back toward the platform. He pushed a button on the radio that was clipped to his uniform. "Dispatch, this is one-four-two-six. I need K-nine. We've got the suspect in the woods, a thousand feet west of the main lodge. He's on foot headed southbound."

Another officer came on the air just as we neared the platform. "I want containment of the four corners of the park. I need two other units to respond."

The platform was strangely empty. Josh and the other counterfeiter were nowhere to be seen. James Ramsey leaned against the Weigh House door, touching a bloody spot on one lip, but otherwise unconcerned.

"Hey, guys," he said, "as soon as Josh could get on his feet, he took off after you."

"What happened here?" I asked.

"We shoved the first guy in there." Ramsey jerked his head backward, to indicate the Weigh House behind him. "So I stayed to make sure he didn't get out before the cops showed up. Josh is still out there, looking for you."

A worried expression crossed the officer's face. "We've got K-nine out there tracking this guy. I hope your friend doesn't get in the way."

But at that moment, Josh burst out of the darkness, bloodied and bruised—his nose resembled a squashed tomato—and saw us. A relieved grin spread across his face.

"I was afraid the other counterfeiter would find you guys first," Josh said.

"He did," I commented.

Josh's eyes widened, but before he could question me, the police officer broke in. "They've got him. K-nine took him down. I'll just hang tight until my partner gets here, and we'll get this other fellow out of your hair too."

"Does that mean we can go home?" Robyn looked as tired as I felt.

The officer glanced at her weary face. "Sure. Leave your contact information with me, and I'll be in touch. I have some questions, but they can wait until morning."

"Come on, kids. I'll take you home," Josh said. "You're done."

"Gantz to the push start position," boomed the announcer's voice.

"Go, Josh!" Robyn called. We were standing on the side of the bobsled track as close to the start as we could get. Josh gave us a thumbs-up, shook his legs to loosen his muscles and pulled on his helmet. He was wearing head-to-toe tight spandex like all of the bobsledders and seemed oblivious to the below-zero temperature.

We, however, were freezing. Again.

"Man, it's cold!" Nick stuffed his gloved fingers under the armpits of his jacket. "Why hasn't someone invented summer bobsledding?"

"Because they need *ice*, Nick," Robyn said.

"Ice is overrated," Nick answered. We watched as Ramsey approached the sled. Ramsey clapped Josh on the shoulder and then thumped him on the helmet. "Good luck, man," he said.

"Same to you," Josh replied. After the night of the stakeout, Josh and Ramsey had become, if not friends, at least, friendlier. Ramsey had risked a lot by jumping into the fight and Josh knew it. If we hadn't found Ramsey that night, who knows what might have happened to Josh.

I didn't like to think about it.

Which brings us to the reason we were back at Olympic Park, freezing our backsides off, yet again. It was the National trials.

The winning bobsledders would be off to compete at the World Cup. Courtney, Robyn, Nick and I were there to cheer Josh *and* Ramsey on.

"Way to go, Josh!" I yelled as Josh and his brakeman took their positions beside the sled. They gripped the handles of the sled, swung it back and forth in a smooth rhythm, and then they dug in their cleats and pushed the sled forward with all their might.

"Go-go-go-go-GO!" we yelled. Josh and his brakeman leaped into the sled. The brakeman tucked his head down as the sled picked up speed.

"Bob in track!" boomed the announcer. We watched as the sled rounded the first curve. The seconds flashed on the clock above us.

"You think Josh'll make the team?" Nick asked.

I shrugged. "I don't know. But at least his sled isn't weighted down with a bunch of fake Euros." Josh and Ramsey were both trying for a spot on the National team. Only one of them would make it. But I guessed in the end what mattered most was that both of them were here today to compete.

"I think we should celebrate no matter what happens," Robyn declared. "Hey, look, isn't that a fifty-dollar bill on the ground over there?" She pointed to the side of the track.

I felt my stomach sink. Oh, no, not again, I thought. Robyn grinned.

"Gotcha!" she joked.

Michele Martin Bossley is the best-selling author of many childrens' books including *Swiped* in the Orca Currents series and *Jumper* and *Kicker* in the Orca Sports series. Michele lives in Calgary, Alberta.